GOODBYE, HELLO

A FOSTER CARE STORY OF RELINQUISHMENT

by Anber & Emily Christensen
editing & design by Nathan Christensen

HWC
PRESS

I was just a year old

When I came to this house.

I was hungry, and tired,

And scared as a mouse.

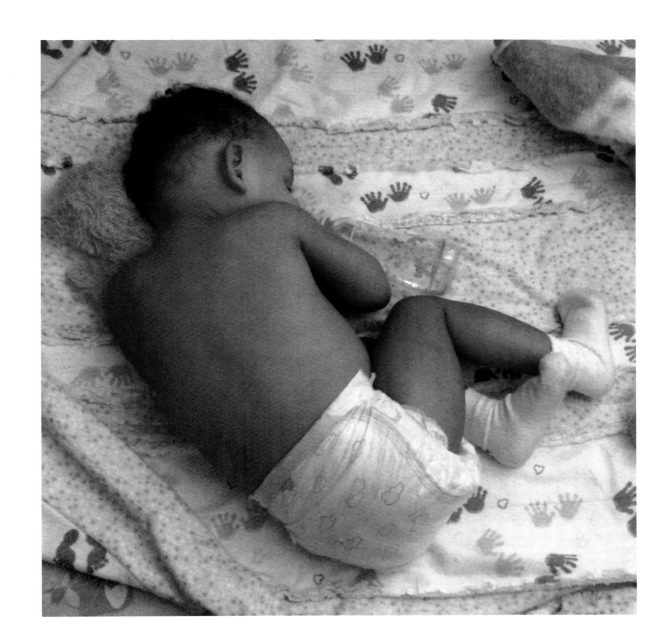

The policemen had pulled me

from all that I knew,

From my not-sober mom,

And her not-safe friends, too.

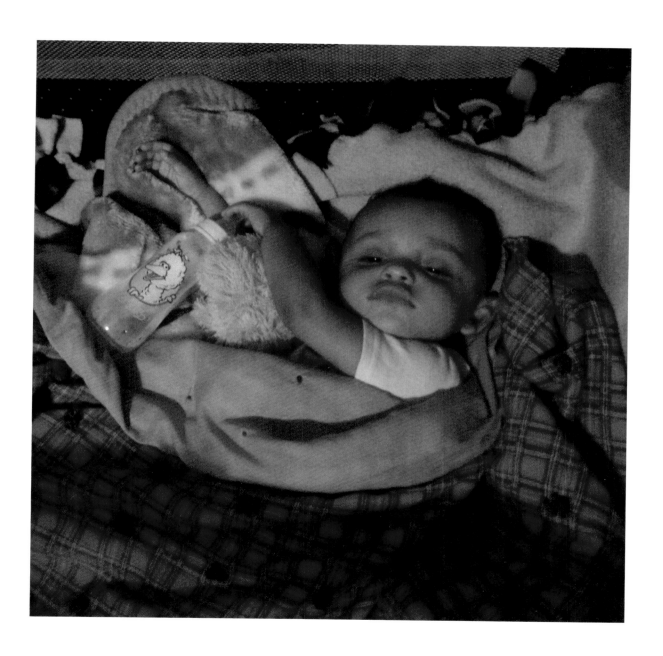

Diapers and anger

Were all that I brought.

My life had been hard,

So I got mad a lot.

I couldn't yet say

What I needed in words.

Instead, I would scream,

And I screamed till it hurt.

But here in this house,

With not-Mom and not-Dad,

I started, for once,

To feel things weren't so bad.

I met this new brother,

All freckles and glee.

He said he'd been locked

In a car, just like me.

There were other kids, too.

Some would stay, some would go.

So many goodbyes.

So many hellos.

And then there were grown-ups

Who came to the door:

Therapists, advocates,

Lawyers, and more.

My caseworker tried

To help Mom stay on track

With steps that were needed

To let me come back.

She said she'd plan visits

For me and my mom.

That thought made me feel

Every feeling but calm.

Each week we would wait

At a park that we knew,

To see if this week

My mom would come, too.

Some weeks she did come.

She would even bring gifts.

She would tell me she loved me,

And give me a kiss.

Then I would come home,

And my red-headed buddy

Would help me calm down

When my feelings got muddy.

Time kept on passing.

I grew, and I grew.

And Mom didn't finish

The things she should do.

This home was becoming

More normal than not.

And my not-Mom-and-Dad?

I loved them a lot.

More foster kids came.

(Hello, and goodbye!)

Most of them moved on in time,

But not I.

My favorite brother

Stayed here with me, too.

In time there were others—

We made quite a crew.

We felt safe together.

No hitting, just hugs,

Where no one went hungry,

And no one used drugs.

One day, my caseworker

Came with a report

Of something important

That happened at court.

My mom signed a paper

In front of a judge,

After more than a year

Of refusing to budge.

"Relinquish" they called it—

A big fancy word,

With more letters in it

Than I'd ever heard.

It meant Mom was tangled

In things that weren't good,

But she wanted to give me

The best life she could.

It meant that she loved me,

But knew, even so,

The time had arrived

For letting me go.

It meant staying put,

And starting to heal,

And that my foster parents

Could become the real deal.

I still miss my mom.

I'm always her kid.

But I'm glad that she made

The hard choice that she did.

Goodbye to the fear

And the pain of the past.

Hello to tomorrow,

And family at last.

First Printing: 2017

ISBN: 978-1-948088-81-7

HWC Press, LLC
P.O. Box 3792
Bartlesville, OK 74006

housewifeclass@gmail.com
www.housewifeclass.com
@housewifeclass

Ordering Information:

U.S. trade bookstores and wholesalers, please contact HWC Press. Special discounts are available on quantity purchase by corporations, association, educators, and others.

About the typeface:

COOKIT, designed by Sérgio Haruo (https://www.behance.net/sergioharuo)